THE OAK TREE

THE OAK TREE

Laura Jane Coats

Macmillan Publishing Company   New York
Collier Macmillan Publishers   London

Macmillan Publishing Company
866 Third Avenue, New York, NY 10022
Collier Macmillan Canada, Inc.
Printed and bound in Japan
First American Edition

10 9 8 7 6 5 4 3 2 1

The text of this book is set in 14 pt. Janson.
The illustrations are rendered in watercolor.
Library of Congress Cataloging-in-Publication Data
Coats, Laura Jane.
The oak tree.
Summary: Birds, people, bats, and other living
things interact naturally with an oak tree over a
period of twenty-four hours.
[1. Trees – Fiction. 2. Nature – Fiction] I. Title.
PZ7.C6293Oak   1987   [E]   86-18099
ISBN 0-02-719052-8

To
Jon Cal

At six o'clock the sun comes up.
Baby birds in a nest wait for their breakfast.

At eight o'clock a squirrel gathers acorns.
Then he hurries off to hide them.

At ten o'clock a cow wanders by
and pauses to scratch her back.

At twelve o'clock children play croquet
and picnic in the shade.

At two o'clock a cloud brings rain. But before long a rainbow appears, and the sun comes out again.

At four o'clock a boy climbs up among
the branches and looks out over the hillside.

At six o'clock the sun goes down,
and as it does the moon begins to rise.

At eight o'clock a traveler takes off his pack
and rolls out his bed for the night.

At ten o'clock black bats swoop through the sky.
Then off they fly into the darkness.

At twelve o'clock an owl watches
a mouse on the moonlit hill.

At two o'clock a possum family
creeps over the hill and slips away.

At four o'clock the traveler awakes.
Soon he is packed and on his way.

And at six o'clock, as the moon goes down,
the sun comes up to begin another day.